RENEE BEAUREGARD LUTE

Winicker
Wallace

Winicker and the American Boy

ILLUSTRATED BY LAURA HORTON

Calico

An Imprint of Magic Wagon
abdopublishing.com

For Maddie, Simon, and Cecily, who inspire me, for Zach, who encourages me, and for my mom, who's told even her hair stylist about Winicker. –RL

To Dad – whose memory will always encourage me to be brave. –LH

abdopublishing.com

Published by Magic Wagon, a division of ABDO, PO Box 398166, Minneapolis, Minnesota 55439. Copyright © 2018 by Abdo Consulting Group, Inc. International copyrights reserved in all countries. No part of this book may be reproduced in any form without written permission from the publisher. Calico™ is a trademark and logo of Magic Wagon.

Printed in the United States of America, North Mankato, Minnesota.
102017
012018

THIS BOOK CONTAINS RECYCLED MATERIALS

Written by Renee Beauregard Lute
Illustrated by Laura Horton
Edited by Heidi M.D. Elston
Art Directed by Laura Mitchell

Publisher's Cataloging-in-Publication Data

Names: Lute, Renee Beauregard, author. | Horton, Laura, illustrator.
Title: Winicker and the American boy / by Renee Beauregard Lute; illustrated by Laura Horton.
Description: Minneapolis, Minnesota : Magic Wagon, 2018. | Series: Winicker Wallace
Summary: Winicker Wallace is delighted to learn that Mademoiselle Bennett's nephew will be
    joining her class. His name is Roger, and just like Winicker, he's American! Winicker
    volunteers to show Roger all of the things she's learned to love about Paris, but Roger isn't
    interested. He would rather disrupt Mademoiselle's class, play mean tricks on Mirabel
    Plouffe, and get Winicker and Mirabel into more trouble than they've ever imagined. When
    it appears Roger has gone too far, Winicker learns the importance of standing up for herself
    and her friends, and that telling an adult is not the same as tattling.
Identifiers: LCCN 2017946558 | ISBN 9781532130489 (lib.bdg.) | ISBN 9781532131080 (ebook) |
    ISBN 9781532131387 (Read-to-me ebook)
Subjects: LCSH: School children--Education--Juvenile fiction. | Bullying in schools--Juvenile fiction. |
    Assertiveness in children--Juvenile fiction. | Humorous Stories--Juvenile fiction.
Classification: DDC [FIC]--dc23
LC record available at https://lccn.loc.gov/2017946558

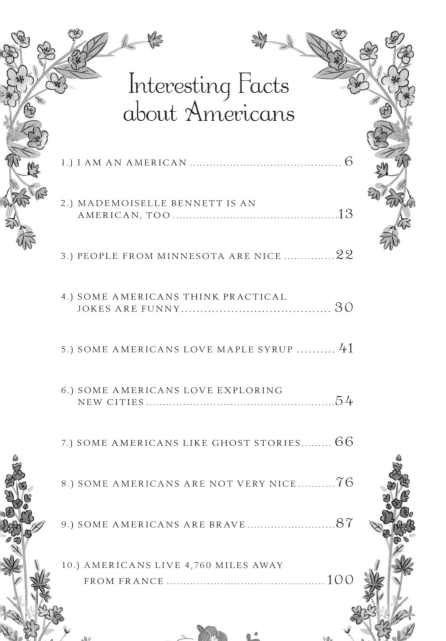

Interesting Facts about Americans

Dear Reader,

I don't know your actual real name, so just pretend your name is in the place where I wrote "Reader."

There are some French words in this book, because this book takes place in Paris. When you see a French word that you don't know, just flip to the back of the book! There is a glossary back there that will tell you what *bonjour* and *merci* mean, and lots of other French words, too.

I know what you are thinking. "Wow, thank you so much! That is really helpful."

You're welcome. I hope you enjoy this very amazing and hilarious story.

Love,
Winicker

One

Today is the first day of spring! Springtime in Paris is the best time in Paris.

My Grandma Balthazar says it's the best because the cherry trees are covered in fluffy pink blossoms.

Mom says it's the best because of all the new spring clothes. She runs the Paris office of a fashion website. In the winter, Mom's website sells boring black boots and long coats. In spring, it sells pale pink shoes and yellow dresses.

Dad says it's the best because he can spend hours writing his book on an open terrace with a cup of espresso. Which I guess is different from spending hours writing his book in the kitchen with a cup of espresso.

I think it's the best because my teacher said she has an exciting surprise for us on the first day of spring. That's today, by the way!

"What do you think it is?" I ask my FBFANDN (French best friend and next door neighbor) Mirabel Plouffe. We are walking to school together.

Mirabel Plouffe sniffs the air. "To me, it smells like hyacinths. That is my very favorite flower, and—"

"No, Mirabel Plouffe," I say. "I don't mean the smell. I mean the surprise. What do you think Mademoiselle Bennett's surprise is?"

"Mm," says Mirabel Plouffe. She stops walking for a second and blinks at the sun. "Maybe it is a very interesting assignment? Maybe it will be a research project and we will visit one of the historic bibliothèques in Paris—"

"NO, Mirabel Plouffe," I say. "Mademoiselle Bennett said she has a surprise for us. She didn't say she has a punishment or a homework assignment for us."

Mirabel Plouffe frowns a little. She loves homework assignments.

"Maybe it's a class pet," I say. "Like a hamster!"

Mirabel Plouffe is still frowning. "I hope it is not a hamster. I do not like rodents. I like cats. Or birds! I love des oiseaux. I will take you to Marché aux Oiseaux one day—the Sunday Bird Market. It is remarkable to see!"

Mirabel Plouffe likes things like watching the news and playing the clarinet and going to bird markets. I don't like any of those things, but I do like Mirabel Plouffe.

"Maybe the surprise is a pizza party," I say. "We used to have those at my old school in Three Rivers. Mrs. Autumn-Robert would order us a pizza and pass around napkins. Everybody got pizza grease on their jeans by the end of the party."

Mirabel Plouffe looks down at her uniform skirt. "Maybe it will be something less messy," she says.

"Maybe."

We walk the rest of the way to school along a row of bright green trees. It isn't cold, but the breeze makes my face and hands chilly. I pull the sleeves of my uniform sweater down over my hands. I smell the air. Mirabel Plouffe is right. It smells like hyacinths. Or some kind of flower, anyway. I don't know. I'm not a flower expert.

When we get to room 3A, my desk cluster looks different. Our desks are in groups of four. Usually there are three other people at my cluster. My FBFANDN Mirabel Plouffe, our friend Amal Aziz, and our not friend Maizy Durand.

Maizy Durand makes fun of my silver hair, which is silver because of an incident with Grandma Balthazar's hair dye. She also makes fun of my name. She makes fun of Mirabel

Plouffe and Amal, too. That is why she is our not friend.

Today, Amal is sitting at our desk cluster, but Maizy Durand is not. She is sitting in another desk cluster.

"Maybe that's the surprise," I whisper. "That would be worth a homework assignment." We sit down at our usual desks.

"Why is Maizy Durand sitting over there?" Mirabel Plouffe asks Amal.

Amal shrugs. "She was there when I came in. I do not want to ask her about it. I do not want her to change her mind and move back!"

We all laugh quietly. But not quietly enough, because Maizy Durand looks up at us and scowls.

"It is not fair that everyone else gets to stay in their original assigned seats." She opens her notebook. "But at least now I will not have to listen to you three whisper about annoying things all day long."

"Did Mademoiselle Bennett ask you to move?" asks Mirabel Plouffe.

"She said she has a surprise and some kind of special assignment for you three. She needed an empty desk in your group." Maizy Durand picks up her pen. "Now please excuse me. I am looking forward to you not distracting me in class for once." She sticks out her tongue at me, Amal, and Mirabel Plouffe. Then she begins writing in her notebook.

"The surprise is a special assignment!" says Mirabel Plouffe. Her face is pink with excitement.

"Maybe it is going to be some kind of projet d'art," Amal says. She draws a tiny paintbrush and palette in a corner on the top of her notebook page. Amal is an artist.

Mademoiselle Bennett appears at the front of the classroom. There is a boy with messy blond hair next to her. He is looking at his shoes.

"Bonjour, everyone," says Mademoiselle Bennett. She is smiling even bigger than usual. She tucks a couple of frizzy brown curls behind her ears and adjusts her orange glasses. "I told you I had a big surprise for you today. And here he is! Please say bonjour to my nephew, Roger!"

The whole class says, "Bonjour, Roger!"

Roger looks up for a second. He nods. "What's up?" Then he looks back down at his shoes.

Roger is an American! Just like me and Mademoiselle Bennett! This is a great surprise!

Two

....

MADEMOISELLE BENNETT IS
AN AMERICAN, TOO

Mademoiselle Bennett guides Roger over to our desk cluster.

"Girls," she says. "I hope you don't mind I moved Maizy. I thought the three of you would be excellent seatmates for Roger. Would you mind showing him around?"

"We would be honored," says Mirabel Plouffe. And she looks honored. She is kind of fanning herself with her hand. She doesn't even seem upset that we didn't get a real assignment.

"I'm Winicker," I say to Roger.

"Hey," says Roger. "Aunt Benny told me you're an American, too."

"I am!" I try to think of something really American to say. "I like baseball!"

Baseball is very American. I don't know why I said I like it, though. I don't like baseball. I like baseball snacks. Like hot dogs and popcorn. I wish I'd just said that I like hot dogs and popcorn. I wish I hadn't said anything about baseball.

"Cool," says Roger.

Mirabel Plouffe and Amal are giving me a strange look.

"So why are you in Paris? How long are you staying? What state are you from?" I ask Roger.

I remember that Mirabel Plouffe is from France and Amal is from Iraq. Maybe they don't know what states are.

"There are fifty states in the United States of America," I tell them. "The state I'm from is Massachusetts. A state is like—"

"Yes," says Amal.

"We know what states are," says Mirabel Plouffe.

"I'm from Minnesota," says Roger.

Minnesota is where Mademoiselle Bennett is from, too.

"Hey, what's the deal with your weird silver hair?" asks Roger. "It's awesome."

"Oh, I used my grandmother's hair dye." I'm not sure whether I should be offended. He said it was weird. But he said it was awesome, too.

"Oh man, that gives me a really great idea." Roger says. He has a strange smile on his face. I wonder what that's supposed to mean. I also wonder what he's doing in Paris.

"So why are you in Paris?" I ask.

"My dad said I've been a handful lately. My aunt said I should come stay with her for a couple of months." Roger looks down at his hands. He looks a little sad. "I miss my cats."

I nod. I've been a handful before. Like when I dyed my hair silver and ruined Mom's towels. And when I said a really, really bad word in class and got sent home early. And when my baby brother was almost born at the Eiffel Tower, which was a little bit my fault. I know what it's like to be in trouble.

"Welcome to Paris," says Mirabel Plouffe. Mirabel Plouffe has probably never been a handful in her entire life. "I am sorry you miss your cats. I love cats. But I think you will have a wonderful time here!"

"Paris has the best food," says Amal. "The chocolate! The pastry!"

Amal's parents own a health food and vegan footwear store in Paris called La Nourriture. They don't let Amal have very much sugar.

"Le fromage," says Mirabel Plouffe. "And the crepes. Even the school lunches in Paris are exceptional."

Mirabel Plouffe is right. At my old school in Three Rivers, the food was pretty good. We had sandwich day, which I liked. We also had Salisbury steak day. Salisbury steak isn't really steak. It's a hamburger patty with gravy on it. The salads were always a little soggy, and dessert was usually a container of pudding.

But at my new school, La Petite École Internationale de Paris, the food is great. The salad is never soggy, and the steak is actual steak. Everything is served with a fresh baguette. I bet Roger will like the lunches here.

Amal is drawing a basket of pastries in her notebook. *Grrrmm.* Her stomach is growling. *Grrrmm.* Actually, that's my stomach growling.

I look up at the chalkboard. Mademoiselle Bennett writes the lunch menu in the top right corner of the chalkboard every day. Today it says:

Pork rib in Dijon sauce

Creamed spinach

Baguette

Cucumber salad with crème fraîche

Pear crumble

I can't wait until lunch.

The lunchroom in La Petite École Internationale de Paris has more plants in it than my entire school in Three Rivers. There are little green potted plants lined up on the windowsills. Baskets of flowery plants hang from the ceiling.

Mirabel Plouffe, Amal, Roger, and I walk into the lunchroom together.

"I hope you will sit with us," Mirabel Plouffe says to Roger.

"Sure," says Roger. "Thanks."

We sit down at our usual table in the corner. I sit next to Amal, and Roger takes the empty seat next to Mirabel Plouffe.

At my old school, we used to line up with a tray to get our food. Here, we just sit down.

The tables are already set with plates, bowls, cups, forks, knives, and spoons, just like when it's dinner at home. Then the food comes out in baskets and on platters, and we serve ourselves.

When the lunchroom people bring the food to our table, Amal reaches for the pear crumble. Roger serves himself a pork rib with lots of Dijon sauce, creamed spinach, and salad with extra crème fraîche. I put a baguette, cucumber salad, and pear crumble on my plate. Mirabel Plouffe takes a little bit of everything. She always does that. She says it's polite.

"Can you tell us what Minnesota is like?" Amal asks Roger.

"Yeah, sure," says Roger. "It's pretty great."

Mirabel Plouffe smiles at Roger. "I love to learn about new places. What are the chief exports of Minnesota?"

Roger sticks his finger into some of the Dijon sauce on his plate and studies it.

"I don't know. I guess right now the chief export is me," he says.

I remember feeling sad and homesick like Roger. And I know what to do about it! We'll show Roger all kinds of great things around Paris, and he'll become one of our best friends.

He and I can talk about American stuff sometimes, too. Like baseball.

Well, not baseball. But we can talk about other American stuff. I'll think of something later.

Springtime really is the best time in Paris.

Three

PEOPLE FROM MINNESOTA ARE NICE

"I live next to Saint Paul. That's the capital of Minnesota," says Roger. "It's nice. There are a lot of old houses and a free zoo. You'd like it, Winicker," he says to me. "Because Saint Paul has its own baseball team. The Saint Paul Saints. There's the Minnesota Twins, too."

I wish I'd never said I like baseball. My dad used to watch Red Sox games on TV when we lived in Three Rivers. They were so boring I sent myself to bed early just so I didn't have to watch.

"What foods do you eat at home?" asks Amal.

"Regular food, I guess," says Roger. He dips his finger into his creamed spinach. "We have a lot of wild rice. And burgers with cheese cooked inside instead of outside."

"Cool," I say. I try to imagine a burger with cheese on the inside.

"Maybe someday you guys will visit," says Roger. "You should see it in the summer. It's really cold in the winter, and it snows a lot. But in the summer we have the Minnesota State Fair where you can get a whole bucket of fresh baked chocolate chip cookies. It's a lot of fun."

"A bucket of cookies sounds wonderful," says Amal.

Roger is really nice. Mademoiselle Bennett is really nice, too. I guess people from Minnesota are nice.

Maizy Durand is frowning at us from her lunch table. Maizy Durand is not nice. She's like the opposite of somebody from Minnesota.

Mademoiselle Bennett stands up at her table and claps her hands. "Five minutes, everyone."

That means we have five minutes to finish our lunch and use the bathroom.

Mirabel Plouffe puts her fork down on the napkin next to her plate. "I am finished. I am going to wash my hands." She stands up and turns around.

Amal and I gasp.

On the back of Mirabel Plouffe's uniform sweater, there is a big smiley face painted on with Dijon sauce. It has crème fraîche glasses and creamed spinach hair. Some of the yellow-white sauce is dribbling down Mirabel Plouffe's back. The face looks like it's melting.

"Oh no, Mirabel!" says Amal. "Your sweater!"

Mirabel Plouffe looks down at her sweater.

"The back," I say. "There is food on your back!"

Mirabel Plouffe tries to look over her shoulder. She carefully pulls her sweater over her head.

"Oh no!" She turns very red. "Who could have—?" But then she stops.

Amal and I don't say anything either. We all know who could have. We know who did.

Because our table is in the corner, and no one was anywhere near Mirabel Plouffe's back. No one except Roger.

Mirabel Plouffe looks at Roger, and her face is different than I've ever seen it. Her mouth is turned down at the corners, and her forehead is crinkled up. This must be what Mirabel Plouffe looks like when she's angry.

"Roger, why would you do something so mean?" she splutters. "We have been very friendly to you, and you—"

"Hang on, I wasn't being mean!" says Roger. He looks very surprised and maybe a little hurt. "Practical jokes must be just an American thing, I guess. I didn't know you'd be so mad about it." He shakes his head and looks at his plate.

"What do you mean?" asks Mirabel Plouffe. "You didn't realize I would be angry that you made a mess of my sweater?"

"No!" says Roger. "Back home in America, kids play practical jokes on each other all the time! Right, Winicker?" He looks at me.

Mirabel Plouffe and Amal look at me, too.

"Uh," I say. I don't think I've ever played a practical joke before. "Maybe! I mean, I've heard that sometimes people play practical jokes."

"See?" says Roger. "It's my way of saying I want to be friends."

"I see," says Mirabel Plouffe. She doesn't look as angry. She looks confused. "Well, of course. We can be friends. But please, I would not like to see any more of your practical jokes."

Roger chuckles. "Sure. Friends?" He sticks his hand out. Mirabel Plouffe shakes it.

Amal dips her napkin into her glass of water. "Mirabel, let me help clean your sweater."

I start to dip my napkin into my water. Then I notice Maizy Durand is standing next to me.

"What do you want, Maizy?" I ask.

"You didn't notice your new American friend was smearing food graffiti all over Mirabel's shirt? You girls should pay more attention." She looks at Mirabel Plouffe. "And watch your back." She walks away.

I do not miss sitting near Maizy Durand in school.

Our five minutes are up, and it's time to go back to the classroom. We all line up at the door and wait for Mademoiselle Bennett to lead us there.

"Psst," whispers Roger. "Can you not tell Aunt Benny about the food on Mirabel's sweater? She would tell my dad, and I've been in enough trouble with him lately."

Mirabel Plouffe looks at me and then Amal and then Roger. "I will not tell," she says to Roger.

"Thanks," says Roger. "I knew you would be great friends to have in Paris."

Amal looks at her shoes. I try to smile at Roger, but I still feel bad about Mirabel Plouffe's sweater. Amal and I tried to scrub most of the food off of her sweater. But it is very hard to clean an extra messy sweater with a couple of wet napkins. There is still Dijon sauce, crème fraîche, and mashed potato on her sweater, and now there are tiny shreds of wet napkin, too.

Mademoiselle Bennett walks up behind us.

"Mirabel Plouffe!" she says. "What happened to your sweater?"

Four

SOME AMERICANS THINK PRACTICAL JOKES ARE FUNNY

The thing about Mirabel Plouffe is that she is good all the time. She does her homework. She keeps her room extra clean. She listens to her mother. She is nice to everybody. And she doesn't lie.

When someone doesn't ever lie, and then she tries to, her lie is really bad. Nobody believes it.

"My sweater," says Mirabel Plouffe. "Yes. Well, you asked that we make Roger feel welcome."

"Roger!" says Mademoiselle Bennett. She makes a very disappointed face at Roger. "Did you do this?"

Mirabel shakes her head. "Non, Mademoiselle, you do not understand. Roger did not do this. I did this."

What?

"What?" asks Mademoiselle Bennett. "You did this, Mirabel? But why? And how? How did you get food all over your own back?"

Mirabel Plouffe looks like she is concentrating. She looks like she is taking the hardest math exam of her life.

"I was . . . eating," she says. "At the lunchroom table. With my friends." She motions to me and Amal. "And with my new friend, Roger." She nods toward Roger. "I once read that Americans love practical jokes. And I wanted to make Roger feel welcome. Of course, I did not want to draw a food face on Roger's sweater. It is a brand-new sweater. And maybe Roger is allergic to Dijon. I do not know. So I drew the food face on my own sweater. It was me, Mademoiselle Bennett."

Mademoiselle Bennett narrows her eyes at Mirabel Plouffe. "Mirabel, I still don't understand how—"

"Well, Aunt Benny," says Roger. "Now you know what happened." He rubs his hands together. "Man, I can't wait to get back to the classroom and learn some neat stuff about the natural habitat of some kind of French bird."

"Ho! Roger, I also love birds," says Mirabel Plouffe. "But we are not learning about birds today. Mademoiselle Bennett has written our agenda on the chalkboard. She did not write anything about birds. I would remember if she had!" Mirabel Plouffe gives Roger a big smile.

Roger smiles back. "Birds are pretty cool."

Birds are not cool. But Roger sounds like he means it. For a second I almost believe Mirabel Plouffe ruined her own sweater, even though I know she didn't. It's just hard to believe Roger did either. He seems like a really nice boy.

Mademoiselle Bennett leans down and whispers to Roger. She pokes her glasses into place and crosses her arms.

"Yes, Aunt Benny," Roger mumbles. "I'm trying."

Mademoiselle Bennett nods at Roger and walks to the front of the line. Roger's cheeks are pink, and he looks down at his shoes.

We follow Mademoiselle Bennett down the long hall to our classroom. When we get to the door of room 3A, Roger doesn't look pink anymore. He isn't looking at his shoes anymore, either.

"Hey." He pokes me in the side. "What American things do you miss the most?"

I think for a second. When we first moved to Paris, I missed my best friend Roxanne's fluffernutter sandwiches. But then Roxanne sent me a box with peanut butter and marshmallow fluff inside. Now I can make fluffernutter sandwiches whenever I want.

I used to miss my old shower, because all we have in our Paris apartment is a bathtub. I used to hate baths, but now I bring a book in with me. You can't read a book in the shower, but you can read it in the bath. If you're careful. Sometimes I am not. That's why my copy of *Harriet the Spy* is drying on the windowsill in my bedroom.

Then I remember.

"Cinnamon flavored stuff," I say. "That's hard to find here. I used to love cinnamon candy."

"Cinnamon candy!" says Amal. "That sounds good."

We sit down at our desk cluster.

Roger's eyes light up. "Wait till you see what I've got in my bag."

He unzips his backpack under the desk where Mademoiselle Bennett can't see. Then he pulls out a small clear bag of little red candy.

Cinnamon candy!

Mirabel Plouffe looks nervously around the classroom. "We are not supposed to eat candy during class."

Roger pretends he doesn't hear her. "How about it, Winicker?" He pours some of the candies into his hand and holds it out to me. I take one.

"Amal?" asks Roger. Amal takes five.

"Do you want some, Mirabel?" asks Roger.

Mirabel looks very pale. She shakes her head no. "We really should not eat candy during class," she says.

Roger still acts like he doesn't hear.

I pop the candy into my mouth.

It's so cinnamony! It's so against the rules. It's so . . . hot! It's burning my tongue! I panic. I swallow it. My whole throat feels like it's on fire! I gulp for air.

Amal! Just as I'm about to warn her, she pops all five of hers into her mouth.

"Amal!" I hiss. "These are—"

But Amal knows. Her eyes get really big. She spits the candies into her hand. She breathes

really fast with her tongue out. "What are these?" she asks Roger. She looks furious. I've never seen Amal look furious before.

I stick my tongue out to cool it off.

Roger is holding his hand over his mouth. I can tell he is laughing because his whole body is shaking and tears are coming out of his eyes.

Finally, he calms down. "They're X-plosive Hot Joke Candies," he says. "Aren't they hot?"

"Yes," I say. My voice sounds creaky coming from my burned throat.

"Roger!" says Amal. "This was not funny!"

Roger frowns. "It was pretty funny," he says. "You should have seen your face!"

"It is not funny to hurt someone, or to ruin their clothing," says Amal. She shakes her head.

Roger sighs. "Look, in America—"

"I am certain it is not funny to hurt people or ruin their things in America," Mirabel Plouffe says loudly.

Mademoiselle Bennett looks up from her desk.

"Shh," whispers Roger. "Please. Look, I'm sorry if you're all upset. But it was just a couple of jokes. Don't be mad at me. And please don't get me in trouble with my aunt. My dad will be so mad."

Mirabel Plouffe narrows her eyes at Roger. Amal is still making a very angry face at him, too.

Roger looks worried. He looks like he's sorry. He looks like a kid whose dad sent him all the way across the world because he was mad at him. My mouth still hurts, but I feel bad for Roger. If my parents sent me across the world without them because I was bad, I would feel awful.

"Okay," I say. "We won't say anything."

I don't tell Mom or Dad or Grandma Balthazar or baby Walter about Roger at dinner. I don't want to get him in trouble with anyone.

"You're being unusually quiet this evening, Winicker," says Grandma Balthazar. She hands me a dinner roll. "Is everything okay?"

"I guess so," I say. I put down the roll on my plate next to a small puddle of pasta in cream sauce. The cream sauce reminds me of the Dijon sauce on Mirabel Plouffe's sweater. I wonder what Mirabel Plouffe told her mother when she got home. I wonder if the stains will come out.

"Ugg," says Walter, because he doesn't say "waaah" like other babies.

"You haven't touched your dinner. Is your stomach bothering you?" asks Mom.

My stomach does feel weird. It feels guilty. Like I did something wrong, even though I didn't do anything wrong. And my mouth still stings from the not-cinnamon candy.

"Just a little," I say. "I think I'll go to bed, if that's okay."

Mom and Dad and Grandma Balthazar look at me, and then they look at each other.

"Gee, kiddo," says Dad. "There isn't even a baseball game on TV! You really must not feel good. Get into bed and I'll bring you a glass of ginger ale in a little while."

Dad brings me ginger ale when I'm sick to my stomach. So does Mom, but she stirs all the bubbles out first. It tastes better when Dad brings it to me. He doesn't stir it.

I go to my room and close the door. When I'm sad, I write a postcard to Roxanne, my best friend in Three Rivers.

I sit at my desk and start a new postcard. This one has a picture of une boucherie on it. There are a bunch of dogs sitting outside, staring at the meat in the window.

Dear Roxanne,

There is an American boy in my school now. He likes practical jokes. Why are they called "practical jokes?" I like regular jokes better. Regular jokes are funny. They don't burn your mouth or ruin your sweater or send people to bed early with guilty-feeling stomachs.

Love,

Five

At breakfast the next day, Mom and Dad and Grandma Balthazar and baby Walter and I are all sitting around the table. Grandma Balthazar made a big fruit salad. Dad is scooping some of his fruit onto a piece of toast.

"Hey, Dad," I say. "You're an American. What do you think about practical jokes?"

Dad stops scooping his fruit. "Practical jokes?" he says. "I think they can be really funny!"

Mom raises one eyebrow at him. "Well, sometimes they can be funny. Sometimes they can scare or even hurt people. Those kinds of jokes aren't funny." She stabs a piece of cantaloupe with her fork.

The cinnamon candy prank kind of hurt.

My tongue feels better this morning, though. I wonder how Amal's tongue is. She had five of those awful candies. I only had one.

"I once played the best practical joke of all time on your mom," says Dad. He smiles a big smile and leans back in his chair. "You were just a baby, Winicker. It was April Fools' Day, and—"

"Honestly, Michael," says Mom. Michael is what Mom calls Dad when she's mad at him. "I don't need to relive it."

"Oh! And there was that joke I played on Grandma Balthazar, where—"

"Oh dear, it's just about time for Winicker to leave for school with Mirabel." Grandma Balthazar stands up from the table and hurries to the front door. She holds it open for me. "You won't need a jacket today, Winicker. The weather is going to be lovely."

I swallow the chunk of watermelon in my mouth and hoist my backpack onto my back.

Mom and Grandma Balthazar really don't seem to want to talk about Dad's practical jokes. I wonder if he gave them burning candy.

I wave goodbye to my family and walk the seven steps to Mirabel Plouffe's apartment.

"Winicker!" Mirabel Plouffe looks surprised when she opens her door. "You are early! You are never early." We walk together through the courtyard in front of our apartment building.

"Grandma Balthazar shooed me out the door early," I say. "Dad was talking about practical jokes he used to play, and Mom and Grandma Balthazar didn't want me to hear about them."

Mirabel Plouffe's smile wilts into a frown. "Practical jokes. I do not understand why they are funny."

"How's your sweater?" I ask.

Mirabel Plouffe shakes her head sadly. "My mother is soaking it. She wanted to know what happened, and I lied because I did not want to get Roger in trouble. I never lie, Winicker! I told my mother that I wore my sweater backward and then accidentally dropped food on it. I am not sure she believed me."

I bet Mrs. Plouffe didn't believe it. Mirabel Plouffe never wears her clothes backward. And she never drops food on her clothes, either. Then again, Mirabel Plouffe never lies, so I guess there's a first time for everything.

When we get to room 3A, Mademoiselle Bennett isn't at the front of the room. And Roger isn't at our desk. Amal and Maizy and all of the other students arrive, but still no Mademoiselle Bennett or Roger. Class is supposed to start at 8:40 a.m. It is 8:44.

Amal is drawing in a corner of her notebook. She draws a tiny table and a tiny chair. She draws a tiny café crème and a plate with some kind of pastry on the table. She draws a tiny Mademoiselle Bennett sitting in the chair.

"Maybe she is having a holiday," says Amal. She draws sunglasses on her tiny Mademoiselle Bennett.

Mirabel Plouffe looks very anxious. "Should we send someone to the principal? Should we report that Mademoiselle Bennett is missing?"

Just then, Mademoiselle Bennett walks in. She is wearing a blue rain hat—the kind of hat French women wear to keep rain out of their faces but also to look fashionable. Grandma Balthazar has three different rain hats.

It isn't weird to see women in France wearing rain hats, except when it's not raining. And it isn't raining.

Mademoiselle Bennett looks angry. She looks angrier than I have ever seen her. Roger walks in behind her. He looks like he is trying not to smile. His eyes are kind of twinkly. He looks over at Mirabel Plouffe and Amal and me, and he winks.

"Bonjour, class," says Mademoiselle Bennett. "Roger, sit down."

Usually when Mademoiselle Bennett tells someone to sit down, she says "s'il vous plait," but she does not say that to Roger. She doesn't even say "please."

Roger shrugs and sits down at our desk.

"What happened?" I whisper. "Why are you late?"

Roger smiles. "Poor Aunt Benny. She'd asked me to bring maple syrup with me when I flew out here. I guess it's hard to find in Paris."

Mirabel Plouffe nods. "I love maple syrup. It is very expensive here and not easy to find."

Amal sighs. "I had some once. It was wonderful."

"But your parents don't let you eat sugar! When did you have maple syrup?" asks Mirabel Plouffe.

"When they were away at a health food convention," says Amal. "My Khala stayed with me, and she likes sweets as much as I do!"

"Why did maple syrup make you late?" I ask Roger.

"Because I brought the maple syrup." Roger grins. " But I guess Aunt Benny didn't expect me to put it on the shelf above the bathtub. And I guess she doesn't wear her glasses in the bath. And I guess she accidentally poured maple syrup in her hair this morning." Roger's grin grows.

"What a terrible thing to do!" says Mirabel Plouffe.

"What a waste of maple syrup," says Amal. She shakes her head.

"I thought you were trying to stay out of trouble!" I say.

Roger sighs. "I do want to stay out of trouble. But your story about dyeing your hair made me think of how funny this would be. I didn't really mean for Aunt Benny to shampoo her hair with maple syrup. I thought she'd realize what was in the bottle. Then she'd laugh, and it would just be a harmless prank."

"I see," says Mirabel Plouffe. "It was an accident."

"Yeah!" says Roger. "It was an accident."

I'm not sure whether Mirabel Plouffe believes Roger or not. I'm not sure whether I believe him or not. I don't think Amal even heard what Roger said. She is drawing a picture of a waffle with a little pat of butter on top, dripping with maple syrup.

When it is time for lunch, Mademoiselle Bennett adjusts her rain hat and claps her hands.

"Class, please line up and walk quietly to the lunchroom. Winicker, would you stay behind and talk to me for a moment, please?"

"Oooooh," say a couple of the kids in my class. They think I'm in trouble. Even though I know I didn't do anything wrong, I feel like I'm in trouble. I hate getting asked to stay behind and talk.

Mirabel Plouffe looks at me with very wide eyes as she stands to line up for lunch.

"Bonne chance," she whispers. Even Mirabel Plouffe thinks I'm in trouble.

When everyone leaves the room, I go up to Mademoiselle Bennett's desk. "You wanted to talk to me?" I ask.

"Oh, Winicker." Mademoiselle Bennett sighs. She adjusts her orange-framed glasses and tucks a sticky-looking curl of hair back under her hat.

"I'm worried Roger isn't adjusting to Paris very well. He was getting into trouble back in Minnesota. So my brother sent him here for a change of scenery. But I'm not sure it's really helping." She points to her hat. "Has he been kind to you and your friends? Is he bothering you or playing mean jokes?"

I don't want to tell Mademoiselle Bennett the truth about Mirabel Plouffe's sweater. What if Mirabel Plouffe gets in trouble for lying? And I don't want to tell her about the not-cinnamon candy, because we aren't supposed to eat candy in class anyway.

And I don't want to tell her about the sweater or the candy because Roger is nice. I think. I mean, he seems really sorry that he caused trouble. He said Mademoiselle Bennett's maple syrup hair was an accident. I don't want him to get sent back to Minnesota, or have his dad be disappointed in him.

I know the feeling of when dads are disappointed. It is the worst feeling in the world.

"He's been really nice," I say to Mademoiselle Bennett. "He hasn't played any mean jokes that I can think of." I pretend to think. I look at the ceiling and tap on my chin. "Nope, no jokes."

"Oh, good." Mademoiselle Bennett looks so relieved I almost don't feel guilty for lying. Almost. "I'm so glad I don't have to tell my brother he's acting out in school. As long as he's being a friend to you girls, can I ask a favor?"

"Of course!" I say. Usually Mirabel Plouffe is the one who does favors for Mademoiselle Bennett. She's always offering to clean the chalkboard. It's usually not even dirty.

"Would you girls take Roger somewhere fun? Show him the Paris that you love? That might be just what he needs. And I need an afternoon at the hair salon to take care of this." She tugs her rain hat, but it doesn't come off. It looks like it's glued to her hair with maple syrup.

I get kind of a bad feeling about lying to Mademoiselle Bennett about Roger. Maybe I should have told her about his practical jokes. But she seemed so upset about her hair. And she looked so happy to hear Roger was being good. I don't want to make her sad again.

"Sure," I say. "We'd love to!"

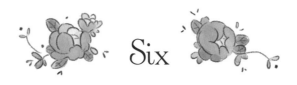

Six

"Why did you agree to spend the afternoon with Roger?" Mirabel Plouffe is distressed. She is biting her thumbnail, which is not very Mirabel Plouffe-ish. She is pacing back and forth in my kitchen, shaking her head. Every once in awhile she says French words I don't know.

Amal and I are sitting at the table. We are waiting for Mademoiselle Bennett to drop Roger off at my apartment. We are going to show him the Latin Quarter. And Mademoiselle Bennett is going to get her hat unstuck from her hair.

"You don't want him to get sent back to America, do you?" I ask her.

"I do not know, Winicker," says Mirabel

Plouffe. "Maybe he would be happier in America. I am sure he misses his family and his friends."

"If he has any friends in America," says Amal. "I do not believe Americans like practical jokes as much as Roger says they do. My tongue is still numb from those awful candies!"

"He may not have friends in America. So we should try really hard to be his friends here in Paris," I say.

I feel bad for Roger. He must be lonely here. He must miss America. I did, when I first moved here. And I had Mom and Dad and Grandma Balthazar with me! Roger just has Mademoiselle Bennett. He must miss his dad and his cats a lot.

Knock knock knock!

Mirabel Plouffe opens the door. "Bonjour!" she says to Mademoiselle Bennett. She nods politely at Roger.

"Bonjour, Mirabel." Mademoiselle Bennett sees me and Amal. "Bonjour, girls!"

"Hi, Mademoiselle Bennett." I stand up. "Hi, Roger. Are you excited to see the Latin Quarter?"

"I guess," says Roger. "Why aren't we going to the Eiffel Tower or someplace I've heard of?"

"Roger," begins Mademoiselle Bennett. She puts her hand to her forehead like she has a headache.

"Because we can walk to le Quartier Latin from here," says Mirabel Plouffe. "My mother works at Shakespeare and Company. She will walk back home with us."

"And some of us have bad memories at the Eiffel Tower," I add.

"And it's a very nice place," says Amal. She joins us near the front door. "There are food stands all over the Latin Quarter, and it smells delicious. There are lights on strings and museums and all kinds of stores with beautiful window displays."

"Great," says Roger. But he doesn't look like he really thinks it sounds great.

"Roger, we're going to have fun!" I say.

I want Roger to have fun. I want us all to be friends so that Mademoiselle Bennett doesn't have to be worried or stuck to her hat. And so Roger's dad doesn't have to get called about Roger being bad. And so I have a real, live American friend from America right here in Paris.

Mademoiselle Bennett, Mirabel Plouffe, Amal, Roger, and I leave for the Latin Quarter. On the way, Mademoiselle Bennett stops at Marlène's, a fancy salon, for her hair appointment. Before she says goodbye and goes inside, she gives Roger a look. Any kid in the whole world would know that look means be good, or else. The rest of us walk the last few blocks to the shops.

My ears and my feet and my nose can all tell at once that we're getting close. There is music playing, and people laughing. The cobbles are bumpy, and I have to pay closer attention to where I'm walking. The air smells like sweet, warm food. It reminds me of the Big E in Massachusetts.

The Big E stands for Eastern States Exposition. It's the big fair for all of the states in New England. I wonder if Roger's Minnesota State Fair is kind of like the Big E. I wonder if the smell of the Latin Quarter reminds him of a fair, too.

I look over at Roger. He doesn't seem interested in the smell. He seems interested in a side street other people are walking down.

"Hey, what's down that way?" Roger asks us.

"That is the way to the Panthéon," says Amal. She shudders. "I have never been there. I am too easily scared."

Roger's eyes get wide. "Why is it scary?"

Mirabel Plouffe laughs and adjusts her backpack on her back. "It is not really scary. It is a very famous church that became a mausoleum after the French Revolution. There is a crypt inside where famous French people are buried."

"Dead French people?" asks Roger.

Amal shudders again.

"Yes, of course," says Mirabel Plouffe.

"We're going," says Roger. "Come on."

Amal bites her lip. She looks down the side street. Then she looks down the street we are walking on. "Wait!" she says. "I am hungry. I am starving! Can we find something to eat first?"

"Good idea, Amal," I say. Maybe if we get some food, Roger will forget about going to a creepy mausoleum. I'm not scared, but I don't want Amal to be. "There's a crepe stand I've been to a couple of times. It has chocolate crepes."

"Mmm," says Amal. "Let's go there."

We find the crepe stand. The list of crepes and prices is on a wooden sign next to the window.

"Whoa, these are kind of expensive," says Roger.

"I have some extra money if you need some," I say. When I first moved to Paris, I never had enough euros for anything because all the money in my piggy bank was American.

"No, don't worry about it. I'll figure it out," Roger says. He smiles that weird smile again.

A man appears in the window of the stand.

"I will have a chocolate crepe," Amal says.

"Me too," I say.

"Moi aussi," says Mirabel Plouffe.

"I want a cheese and potato crepe," says Roger.

Which is strange for two reasons. One is that nobody orders a potato and cheese crepe when they can order a chocolate crepe. The other is that Roger is worried about how expensive the crepes are. But the cheese and potato crepe is the most expensive crepe on the menu.

We all pay for our crepes separately and wait until they are ready.

The man hands me my crepe, and it is almost too warm to hold. My stomach grumbles.

There is a bench next to the crepe stand. Amal and Mirabel Plouffe and I sit to eat our chocolate crepes. Mine is just as delicious as I remember! Roger paces in front of us.

"How is it?" I ask.

"It's pretty good!" Roger says through a mouthful of crepe.

Maybe this day will be great after all. Maybe Roger won't do any more practical jokes.

"Ouch!" yells Roger. He covers his mouth.

"What is wrong?" asks Mirabel Plouffe. She stands up and puts down her crepe on the bench. Mirabel Plouffe likes to be helpful. The man in the crepe stand sticks his head out of his window to look at Roger.

"I bit into something really hard!" says Roger.

He takes his hand away from his mouth. He holds it out to us. There is a shiny coin in his palm. "This was in my crepe!" He holds it up and shows the man in the window.

The man gasps. "Je suis désolé! I do not know how this could have happened! Let me make you another!"

"So I can bite into something else and break a tooth? No thanks!" Roger yells, looking very upset and waving the coin around. "And what about my friends?"

"Here, take your money back. All of you." The man looks very worried. He holds out the euros that Roger paid for his crepe.

"Oh man. My mouth really hurts." He flashes the coin that was in his crepe to me and Mirabel Plouffe and Amal again. Then he tucks it into his pocket. He takes his euros back from the man in the crepe stand and hurries me, Amal, and Mirabel Plouffe away from the window.

The crepe stand takes euros as payment for food, like all of the other places I've eaten in Paris. That's why I don't understand how that coin could have gotten inside Roger's crepe. The coin was an American quarter.

Could Roger have put the quarter into his own crepe? Why would he do something like that? Just to get his money back?

I look back at the man in the window at the crepe stand. His hands are in his hair. He looks very unhappy. He sighs and begins digging through his bowls of crepe fillings. He's obviously looking for other coins. He's making sure this doesn't happen again.

His face reminds me of Mirabel Plouffe's face when Roger smeared food all over the back of her sweater. And Amal's face when Roger gave her those five awful spicy candies. And Mademoiselle Bennett's face when she was late to school and her hat was stuck to her hair. All because Roger had swapped her shampoo with maple syrup.

Actually, Roger has done a lot of not-very-nice things since he got to Paris.

Maybe he did put the quarter in his own crepe.

"Let's go to the Panthéon!" says Roger. He winks at us.

Seven

SOME AMERICANS
LIKE GHOST STORIES

Amal does not want to go to the Panthéon. Her eyes are really big. She keeps squeezing my arm as we walk up to the huge building with tall columns. I'm definitely not scared at all, but I don't want to go either. For Amal's sake. Definitely not mine.

"This is so cool," says Roger. "I bet it's really creepy and haunted by all the dead people inside."

Amal squeezes my arm really, really hard.

Mirabel Plouffe laughs. "Of course it is not haunted," she says to Roger. "There are no ghosts. But there is history! Marie Curie is buried inside! She was the first woman to win a Nobel Prize. She won it twice, in fact—"

"That's great about Mariah Carey," says Roger. "But you're wrong about the ghosts. There are always ghosts where dead people are buried."

"Marie Curie," says Mirabel Plouffe. "Not Mariah Carey. Marie Curie."

Amal shivers. "I would like to wait outside. You can see the Panthéon together, and I will wait here on the steps. I can hold your backpack, Mirabel."

"I can wait with you!" I say. I feel relieved, but not because I was scared. I wasn't scared. I feel relieved that Amal doesn't have to be scared.

"Well okay," says Roger. "I was just hoping that all of us could go in together, since Aunt Benny asked you three to show me around. I guess you could stay here by yourselves. I just hope Aunt Benny won't be mad that we all split up—"

"Fine," I say. "We'll go in with you. But just for a minute." Mademoiselle Bennett just wanted an afternoon to herself. And I said I would show

Roger around. But as we walk up the rest of the steps, I get a cold, tight feeling in my stomach. Mirabel Plouffe is usually right about things. I hope she's right about there not being any ghosts at the Panthéon, too.

We walk inside, past a small tour group. The ceiling is very high. All of the windows let in a lot of light.

"See?" I whisper to Amal. "This isn't so bad." Amal nods.

There are statues and murals all over the walls.

"The building is modeled after the Pantheon in Rome," says Mirabel Plouffe. "Over here is Foucault's Pendulum. It measures the rotation of the earth." She walks us toward a big table in the middle of the floor. There is a big measuring tape around it and a golden ball swinging from a wire above it. A couple of tourists are taking pictures.

I don't see what all the fuss is about. My brother, Walter, is a baby and he has toys a lot more interesting than this.

"To be honest, it's actually a copy," says Mirabel Plouffe. "Not the original."

It isn't even the real thing. Now I really don't see what all the fuss is about.

Amal doesn't look scared anymore. She is looking at a sculpture of a woman in a long robe.

"That is Marianne," says Mirabel Plouffe. She is a symbol of France.

"Neat," says Roger. "Let's go downstairs."

"Downstairs?" I say.

"Where the crypts are," says Mirabel Plouffe. "Voltaire is there. And Victor Hugo, and—"

"We know," says Roger. "Lots of famous dead French people. Let's go."

Amal and I look at each other. She squeezes my arm again. We follow Roger and Mirabel Plouffe to the stairs.

When we get downstairs, it is darker than the main floor. But there are lots of tourists taking photos. And there are some lights along the ceiling.

I practice looking like a person who isn't scared. I read a banner with a picture of a woman named Genèvieve de Gaulle-Anthonioz on it. She was a member of the French Resistance. That's what the banner says.

I nod. "Hmm," I say. "Interesting."

Amal nods too.

We walk to another banner. There is a picture of a man named Victor Hugo on it. The banner says he was a writer. My dad is a writer, too. Maybe he should visit the Panthéon. He can come with Mom and Grandma Balthazar and Walter. I'm visiting it right now, so I probably don't ever need to visit again.

"Look, Mirabel Plouffe," I say. "Here are some interesting facts about Victor Hugo."

Mirabel Plouffe likes interesting facts about things.

"Oui," says Mirabel Plouffe. "And here is the casket where he is buried!" She points to a large gray box next to the banner. There is an actual real dead person in that box.

One of the lights on the ceiling goes out with a pop and we all jump.

I get a creepy crawly feeling all over my skin.

A small tour group walks up next to us. The man leading the group has a white beard and a dark brown suit.

"And that," he says to his group, "is my final resting place."

Amal looks at me. I look at Mirabel Plouffe.

"Did he just say—" I begin.

"I told you," says Roger. "I told you there are ghosts here." His eyes are very wide. He turns to the tour guide. "What's your name, mister?" asks Roger.

The man with the white beard laughs.

"My name is Victor Hugo, son. Have you heard of me?" He points to the name tag pinned on the front of his suit jacket.

It says VICTOR HUGO.

"AAAAAUUUUUGGGGGHHHHHH!" I scream. I take Amal's hand and we run back up the stairs and through the main floor until

we get to the steps outside. Mirabel Plouffe and Roger run after us. When they reach us on the steps, Roger is laughing.

He is laughing so hard he is shaking.

"What's so funny?" I ask. My heart is beating hard. Amal doesn't look as terrified as I feel. She looks annoyed at Roger.

"You thought that was a ghost!" says Roger. "You were so scared! Of a tour guide! Oh man, I wish I'd gotten a picture of your face. That was too good."

My face is burning hot. I clench my fists and grit my teeth. I don't think this is funny at all.

Mirabel Plouffe's head is to one side, and she looks like she feels bad for me. "He was just an actor, Winicker. I am sorry you were so afraid. He was not a ghost. As I said earlier, there are no ghosts at the Panthéon."

"Yes, thank you, Mirabel Plouffe," I snap. "I know there are no ghosts at the Panthéon."

Mirabel Plouffe looks surprised and a little hurt. "I am sorry if I offended. I just wanted to reassure you."

I sigh. "Thanks, Mirabel Plouffe."

Amal looks toward the street. "Let's go to Shakespeare and Company. I don't need to see any more of the Panthéon."

We start walking in silence. I am annoyed at Roger for scaring me. And I am annoyed at myself for being scared. Amal seems annoyed at Roger, too. Mirabel Plouffe is worried that I am annoyed at her, I think, but I'm not. Not really, anyway.

I link arms with her. "Maybe we can get hot chocolate at the café next to the bookstore first," I say. "We can take it with us."

Mirabel Plouffe looks at me like I just grew three heads and one of them has a foot sticking out of its ear. "We cannot bring hot chocolate into the bookstore, Winicker! It is very important to respect the books. What if we spilled?" Her eyes are very wide, like she's seeing the ghost of Victor Hugo.

"Yeah," I say. "That would be terrible."

We walk along the streets, and try not to trip on the cobbles in places where they stick out more. There are little puddles from the last time it rained, and puffy, pink blossoms on some of the trees that line the sidewalk.

The Latin Quarter is one of my favorite places in Paris. Especially in the spring.

"Voilà!" says Mirabel Plouffe. She points to a familiar green building with a stack of books outside and a yellow sign on top that says Shakespeare and Company.

Eight

Mirabel walks into the bookstore like it's a museum full of her favorite things. I guess it kind of is a museum full of her favorite things.

She takes a deep breath. "Is it not the most wonderful smell in the world?" she says.

Roger jams his hands into his pockets. He looks around. "It smells old. Why is it so dark?"

"It is better for the books. Too much natural light will fade them." Mirabel Plouffe looks a little deflated.

Roger kicks at one of the stone tiles on the floor. Mirabel Plouffe crinkles her forehead. She looks either sad or mad. Or both. It's hard to tell, because Mirabel Plouffe is almost never sad or mad.

"Hey, let's look around," I say. "Roger, did you know this is one of the most famous bookstores in the world?"

We walk down a long, narrow aisle of books.

"Really?" says Roger. "Why's it so famous? It's pretty cramped." He squeezes past Amal and knocks a couple of books onto the floor. "See?"

Mirabel Plouffe picks them up. Her forehead is even crinklier. She is definitely mad.

"In Minnesota, we have a bookstore that has chickens and cats and a chinchilla walking around. There are live rats under the floor that you can watch through these see-through tiles. It's the best."

Mirabel Plouffe shakes her head. "Non, I cannot imagine this is true. The cats would eat the chickens, and the books would smell like animals."

"It is true. It's called Wild Rumpus, and the books do not smell like animals." Now Roger's forehead is crinkly. "And Minnesota is a lot better than Paris. And America is a lot better than France!"

Mirabel Plouffe's mouth drops open. Then she closes it. "You are a very rude and awful boy," she says. She turns around and walks down the aisle of books, careful not to let her backpack knock any of the books off the shelves.

Amal leans close to me. "That is the first time I have ever heard Mirabel say something unkind," she whispers out of the side of her mouth. She waits for Roger to follow Mirabel Plouffe down the aisle. "But I am glad she said it. Roger is a very rude and awful boy!"

I nod. I feel kind of sad about it. Maybe Roger really is awful. On the other hand, I remember feeling the way he feels. About America and about Paris. When I first got here, I thought everything and everybody was awful. I missed my home so much. Roger must miss home, too.

But what Mirabel Plouffe said is true. He's being rude and awful right now.

We follow Roger and Mirabel Plouffe into another room of Shakespeare and Company. This one just has books all around the walls. There is room for the four of us to stand in the middle of the floor.

"Look," says Roger. "I'm sorry about what I said. But you shouldn't go around saying bad things about places you've never been."

Mirabel Plouffe's face looks more like her usual not-mad face. "I am sorry, too. You are right, Roger. I should not have said your bookstore must smell like animals. But you must understand this bookstore is like home to me! My mother has always worked here. I grew up here!"

Roger nods. "Let me make it up to you." He looks around desperately for something to do and then his eyes light up. "I'll carry your backpack!" he says and picks it up with both hands.

"No, that is not necessary," Mirabel Plouffe protests.

Before she can say anything else, a face with two long, red braids appears in the doorway. It is not a smiling face. It is Maizy Durand's face.

"Are the four of you having fun?" she asks. She doesn't look like she wants us to answer. She crosses her arms.

Amal looks at me and raises her eyebrows. I raise mine back.

"Hey, you're in our class, right?" asks Roger. He doesn't know Maizy Durand is awful yet.

"Right. You took my seat," says Maizy Durand.

Everyone is quiet for a few seconds. The room is starting to feel even warmer and smaller than it did a few minutes ago.

Roger looks uncomfortable. He walks over to a little table at the end of the shelf. He puts down Mirabel Plouffe's backpack and picks up a book with a shiny gold peacock on the cover.

He flips through a few pages and puts it back. A moment later, he picks up the same peacock book and flips through it again. Either he really likes peacocks, or he wants to avoid this conversation as much as I do.

"I have not seen you here before," Mirabel Plouffe says to Maizy Durand. "I am here a lot. My mother—"

"Yes, I know. Your mother works here," says Maizy Durand. "Do you think I don't listen? I sit right next to you every day. At least, I did until last week."

For a moment, I think Maizy Durand is going to say something else. But then she brushes past us. "Excuse me. Some of us are here to look at books, not just take up space," she says to Roger.

Roger clearly doesn't know what to do, so he just stands there. He puts down the peacock book and backs away slowly from the table. He looks like a person trying not to make a bear angry.

"Should we go find your mom?" I ask Mirabel Plouffe. I am relieved we have an excuse to get away from Maizy Durand before anything else happens. I am also a little relieved that we'll have a grown-up with us on the way home. Roger probably won't scare anybody or put quarters in crepes if there is a grown-up with us. Plus, next to Maizy Durand, Roger doesn't seem so bad.

"Oui," says Mirabel Plouffe, "she is at the desk. Follow me."

We walk back through the tight rows of books toward the room with the checkout desk. Mirabel Plouffe suddenly gasps. "Oh no, my backpack!"

Roger looks embarrassed. "I left it back there," he says. "I said I'd carry it, so I guess I have to go back to get it." He disappears back the way we came.

When Roger returns, he has the backpack.

"Sorry that took a minute. Maizy was still back there. She seems pretty nice. Maybe you guys should give her a chance. I bet she'd enjoy a good joke."

Maizy Durand probably would enjoy one of Roger's awful jokes. I really hope he doesn't have any more planned tonight. I just want to get out of here and go home. Surely he's learned his lesson at this point.

"Thank you for your help, but I can carry my backpack," Mirabel Plouffe says to Roger. He's still smiling as he helps her put it on.

Mrs. Plouffe is at the checkout desk stamping a picture of William Shakespeare on the inside of a book for a customer with a swishy pink skirt. When the customer leaves, Mrs. Plouffe sees us standing across the room.

"Mirabel!" she says. Her face lights up when she sees Mirabel Plouffe. And Mirabel Plouffe's face lights up when she sees Mrs. Plouffe. They're like a mother and daughter from a children's movie about a mother and daughter. "Bonjour, everyone! It must be time to walk home. I will just finish a couple of things here, and then I will meet you outside!"

Roger walks out first.

There is a pink tree in bloom on the sidewalk right outside Shakespeare and Company. Everyone who walks under it looks up and sips their coffee and smiles. Roger is smiling up at it now. Amal and I smile at it on our way out, too. Maybe everything isn't so bad with Roger. He said he was sorry. And it's springtime in Paris, and everything smells good and fresh. And—

Eeee eeee eeee eeee!

Something is making a very high-pitched, loud sound.

Eeee eeee eeee eeee!

I look back at the doorway of Shakespeare and Company. Mirabel Plouffe is standing there. She looks confused.

"Mirabel Plouffe?" I say. "What is—"

"Mirabel," says a large man in a dark suit. "Ho! Our new security device must be broken. You are the first person to set it off!" The man chuckles. "Try to walk through the door again, s'il vous plaît."

Mirabel Plouffe walks through again.

Eeee eeee eeee eeee!

The man shakes his head. He taps on his moustache. "I am embarrassed to ask you, Mirabel, but would you open your backpack?"

Mirabel Plouffe turns very red. Mrs. Plouffe hurries up to the man and Mirabel Plouffe. She looks as confused and embarrassed as Mirabel Plouffe does.

Mirabel Plouffe unzips her backpack. The man in the suit reaches his hand inside and pulls out a book. A book with a shiny gold peacock on the cover. The same book Roger pulled off the shelf.

The man narrows his eyes at Mirabel Plouffe.

Nine

SOME AMERICANS ARE BRAVE

Mirabel Plouffe is even redder, and she shakes her head at the man and Mrs. Plouffe.

"Non! This is not my—I did not put this book in my backpack!"

Amal whispers in my ear. "She could not have stolen it. Mirabel would never steal!"

Amal is right. But Mirabel Plouffe would never lie either. Maybe her one lie set her off down a dark road. And now she's going to have a life of crime. All because she tried to protect Roger. It's so unfair.

Maizy Durand joins us. She has a mean smile on her face. I bet she'd just love it if Mirabel Plouffe got in trouble. Maizy Durand is awful.

The man in the suit shakes his head at Mrs. Plouffe. "If your daughter is taking books without paying for them, she cannot come and visit you here."

Mrs. Plouffe looks furious. "Ma fille would never take a book without paying for it!"

The man puffs out his chest. "She just did!" He shakes the book at Mrs. Plouffe. "If you insist that the truth is not the truth, and you bring thieves to this bookstore, I will not have you working here anymore!"

Mirabel Plouffe's eyes are full of tears. Mrs. Plouffe looks like she is going to cry, too.

I look at Roger. His eyes are wide and he is watching everything that is happening. He isn't smiling anymore. He looks a little worried.

Maybe he looks worried because he put that book in Mirabel Plouffe's backpack. I don't know it for sure, but if I were a detective, the clues would add up.

Roger likes practical jokes.

Roger likes practical jokes that aren't funny.

Roger just had an argument with Mirabel Plouffe.

Mirabel Plouffe would never ever steal a book. Or anything else.

Roger was alone with Mirabel Plouffe's backpack for a minute.

I saw Roger holding that book before it ended up in Mirabel Plouffe's backpack.

That last two clues are probably the most important.

What is going to happen to Roger if I tell the man in the suit about the last clues? Will the police come? Will Roger go to French prison? The Bastille is a French prison. Will Roger go to the Bastille? Will he be kicked out of France? Will the man in the suit call Mademoiselle Bennett?

Actually, that last one is probably the one that would happen.

My stomach does a flip-flop because I don't like telling on other people. And I especially don't like telling on other people when they are right there.

But I do like Mirabel Plouffe. And I like justice. So I have to do a brave thing that makes me feel a little sick. "Mirabel Plouffe did not steal that book," I say.

The man in the suit squishes his eyebrows together. "And how do you know that?"

Roger is looking at me. It would have been nice to have an American friend in Paris who I could talk to about American things. But I would rather have a good friend in Paris. My good friend is my FBFANDN Mirabel Plouffe. And she is in trouble. And I'm the only person who can help.

"I know she didn't steal the book because I saw Roger holding that exact book right after he had an argument with Mirabel Plouffe. And he plays mean practical jokes all the time. He drew a face made out of food on Mirabel Plouffe's sweater a couple of days ago."

Mrs. Plouffe looks at Mirabel Plouffe. "Mirabel! You told me that you wore your sweater backward and accidentally dropped food on it. I thought the story sounded strange, but you have never lied to me before!"

Mirabel Plouffe looks down at her shoes. "I know. I am sorry I lied, Maman."

"Why did you lie?" asks Mrs. Plouffe.

Mirabel Plouffe wipes away a tear. "We thought Roger wanted to be friends. And we did not want to disappoint Mademoiselle Bennett. She is his aunt. She asked us to show Roger around."

"We wanted to be his friend," I say. "We thought all of the jokes were just him trying to be friendly."

"But we do not think that anymore," says Amal.

Everyone looks at Roger. Me and Amal and Mirabel Plouffe and Mrs. Plouffe and the man in the suit. Roger looks very sad.

"I was just trying to be friendly," says Roger. "I miss my old friends in Minnesota, and that's what we used to do together. Practical jokes. Sometimes they got us in trouble, but we always

had fun. But I would never frame somebody for stealing a book! That's illegal! You think I want to end up in French prison or something? Plus, that's just really mean." Roger shakes his head. "I didn't put that book in Mirabel's bag. I promise. I'd never do that."

Mirabel Plouffe kind of smiles at Roger, but her smile looks even sadder than her frown did. If Roger didn't put the book in Mirabel Plouffe's bag, then Mirabel Plouffe is going to be in a lot of trouble.

"I put the book in Mirabel's bag," says Maizy Durand.

We all gasp. This is just exactly like those old black-and-white detective movies Dad likes to watch.

Mirabel Plouffe's mouth drops open. "You? Maizy, why? Why would you do this?"

Mrs. Plouffe squeezes Mirabel Plouffe's shoulder. Mirabel Plouffe looks shocked and relieved at the same time.

"You seemed to be having fun spending time together outside of school. And you never invite me. Never. And when Mademoiselle Bennett moved me in class so Roger could take my seat, I heard you. You were all so happy I wasn't going to sit with you anymore. How do you think that made me feel?" Maizy Durand's eyes are full of tears. I have never seen Maizy Durand cry before.

I feel pretty terrible. "I guess I didn't think—"

"You didn't think I needed friends? You didn't think it would hurt my feelings to hear you talking about how awful I am?" A tear slides down Maizy Durand's face. She wipes it away with her arm.

"I'm sorry, Maizy Durand," I say. And I really feel sorry.

"I'm sorry, too," Mirabel Plouffe and Amal say at the same time.

"Uh . . . and I'm sorry I took your seat," says Roger. He shrugs.

"You did this, little girl?" says the man in the suit. "Well, then we are going to have to call your parents. I will let you tell them what happened."

Maizy Durand nods and begins to follow the man into the store.

"Wait," I say. Maizy Durand turns around to look at me. "Maybe we can all go somewhere together next weekend. Mirabel Plouffe wants to show me some kind of Sunday bird market. And probably write a report on it."

"Oh yes!" says Mirabel Plouffe. "Let's all go to the bird market next weekend!"

Maizy Durand rolls her eyes. "That's the most ridiculous thing I've ever heard." She sighs. "But thank you for inviting me. I'd like to go."

"We will look forward to it," says Mirabel Plouffe. "And Maizy, thank you for telling Monsieur Winsor about what you did. I know it could not have been easy. You have saved my mother's job!"

"And kept Roger out of the Bastille," I add.

"Oui, thank you, Maizy," says Mrs. Plouffe.

Maizy Durand nods at all of us and follows Monsieur Winsor into the bookstore.

Then I notice how sad Roger still looks. I felt brave when I told about how I thought he put the book in Mirabel Plouffe's backpack. I might have been brave, but I was also jumping to conclusions.

I wish I had been brave a couple of days ago, when Roger drew the food face on Mirabel Plouffe's back. Or when he gave me and Amal those candies. Or when he pretended to find a quarter in his crepe. Or when—

Well, anyway. I should have been brave and said something all of those times. But I said something now, and it happened to be the wrong thing. Now Roger looks almost as hurt as Maizy Durand did.

"I'm sorry I thought you put that book in Mirabel Plouffe's bag," I say.

Roger nods and looks down. "I understand why you did. I guess I've been pretty rotten to you guys since I got here. I really didn't mean to be. That's just how I joke around with my friends back in Minnesota."

"Maybe we should think of some practical jokes that don't hurt people or ruin their things," I say.

"Okay," says Roger. "I'm open to new kinds of practical jokes. Anyway, should we all walk back to your apartment? Aunt Benny will be there soon to pick me up."

"Oui," says Mrs. Plouffe. "I will walk you—"

"Wait." I feel my braveness happen again. "Roger, did you put that quarter in your own crepe back at the crepe stand?" I ask.

Roger's eyes get wide. "Yeah. But I did it for you guys, too! We all got our money back! Nobody got hurt."

"The man in the crepe stand got hurt!" says Mirabel Plouffe. She covers her mouth with her hands. "This is true? I ate a stolen crepe? I really am a thief!" Her face looks kind of gray. Mrs. Plouffe hugs her.

"Let's go back to the crepe stand," I say. "We can give the man all of the money we owe him. And you can apologize."

Roger takes a deep breath. He straightens up. He looks like he is trying to feel brave, too. "Okay. Let's do it."

Mrs. Plouffe smiles encouragingly at Roger. "Let's go."

Ten

The man at the crepe stand wasn't even very angry when Roger told him the truth. He seemed kind of relieved there weren't coins in his potatoes. We paid him again, and he was nice about the whole thing. He even let Amal have a free sample of a new caramelized banana crepe he is inventing.

So that's why we are all surprised at how mad Mademoiselle Bennett is. She is standing in my kitchen. Her hair looks much shorter than it did before, but very stylish. She looks like the spring dress models on Mom's fashion website. And there's no hat glued to her hair with maple syrup. Her face is mad and sad at the same time.

"Roger, I'm going to need to tell your dad you're having a hard time adjusting here." She puts a hand on his shoulder and guides Roger to the door.

"I know," says Roger. He raises his eyebrows at me, Amal, and Mirabel Plouffe. "Wish me luck, guys."

I do wish him luck. Roger isn't so bad after all.

On Monday, Mademoiselle Bennett and Roger are on time for class. Mademoiselle Bennett winks at me and Amal and Mirabel Plouffe. Then she writes the day's lesson and menu on the chalkboard.

Roger sits in his seat at our desk cluster. I expected him to be sad after getting in trouble with his dad. But he smiles at us and sets his notebook and pen on the desk. Then he turns to look at the chalkboard.

I look at Mirabel Plouffe. She looks at Amal. Amal looks at me. We all want to know what happened when Roger's dad found out about his practical jokes. Is he in big trouble?

"Hey," I whisper to Roger.

He doesn't hear me. Or he's pretending not to hear me. I pretend I don't care. I try to study the puffy white cat on my folder. Mirabel Plouffe gave me this folder when I first moved to Paris. The cat is wearing a jeweled collar. It has big blue eyes and a little pink nose. I wonder if Mom, Dad, and Grandma Balthazar would let me get a cat.

I have to know what happened.

"I said hey," I whisper a little louder.

He's still pretending he doesn't hear me.

I would think of a really good and hilarious name for my cat. Like Clawdia. Or Jennifur.

"I said HEY!" I whisper-yell.

"Winicker," whispers Mirabel Plouffe. "Shhh. You are going to get us all in trouble!"

Roger finally turns away from the chalkboard. He looks at us with a twinkle in his eye. "What's up?"

"Speaking of trouble," Amal whispers. "What happened when your dad found out about everything, Roger?"

"Yes, what did happen, Roger?" asks Mirabel Plouffe.

"He got mad, but mostly at himself for sending me here. He bought me a one-way ticket back home. Today is my last day at your school," whispers Roger. "I'm going home to Minnesota tomorrow morning."

"Ohhh," Mirabel Plouffe, Amal, and I whisper all at once.

"Are you going to be grounded when you get there?" I ask.

Roger shrugs. "Yeah. But I'd rather be grounded at home than sent away to another country. So I guess everything worked out okay."

I feel sad Roger is leaving, because it would have been nice to have an American friend here. Especially now that I know he really was just trying to be friendly. I feel a little relieved there won't be any more practical jokes. And I feel happy for Roger. He missed Minnesota a lot.

"Have a safe trip home!" whispers Mirabel Plouffe. "Behave on your flight. And drink water."

Amal nods. "Good luck with your dad, Roger." She draws a little airplane in a corner of her notebook.

"Thanks," says Roger. "And, uh, I really am sorry about everything."

"It's okay," says Amal. And Mirabel Plouffe and I nod.

"We know you are," I say.

Mirabel Plouffe and I walk home together at the end of the day. The breeze feels good on my face. It rained while we were in school, so everything smells sweet and clean, like spring. Mirabel Plouffe hops over a shallow puddle. I splash through it with my rain boots.

She leans down and smells a couple purple flowers. "Hyacinths," she says. "My favorite."

"Mirabel Plouffe," I say. "Remember when you said you liked cats?"

"Oui!" says Mirabel Plouffe. "I love cats."

"What do you think about the name Clawdia?"

Mirabel Plouffe throws her head back and laughs.

I'm glad Roger went back to the home he loves. But I wish he could have stayed a little longer. When you get used to Paris, it is impossible not to love it.

Mirabel Plouffe squints up at the sun. "It is a beautiful day, non?"

"Oui," I say. "A very beautiful day."

PRACTICAL JOKE IDEAS

Dear Roger,

We hope you are glad to be home in Minnesota. Your friends in Paris brainstormed some amazing practical joke ideas that won't hurt anyone or make them mad at you.

1.) Pour some cereal and milk into a bowl, and then put it in the freezer. The next morning, tell your dad you made breakfast. He won't be able to stick his spoon into the cereal because it will be frozen solid!

2.) Get five or six paper cups. Turn the cups upside down and write things like "HUGE SPIDER UNDER HERE" and "EVEN HUGER SPIDER UNDER THIS ONE" on them. Leave them upside down around the house. Your dad will think there are really spiders under the cups!

3.) Stick pairs of googly eyes on all of the fruit. It'll be hilarious. Trust us.

4.) Call your cats by each others' names. It will be very funny. (This one is Mirabel Plouffe's idea. Just so you know, me and Amal and Maizy do not think it is funny. But we didn't want to hurt Mirabel Plouffe's feelings.)

Your friends,

Winicker, Mirabel Plouffe, Amal, and Maizy, who sits with us again.

Winicker Wallace's

Bibliothèques: Libraries

Bonjour: Good day

Bonne chance: Good luck

Une boucherie: A butcher shop

Café crème: Coffee with cream

Crème fraîche: Fresh cream

Le fromage: Cheese

Ho!: Oh!

Je suis désolé!: I am sorry!

Ma fille: My daughter

Maman: Mother

Marché aux Oiseaux: Bird Market

Moi aussi: Me too

Non: No

La Nourriture: The Food

Des oiseaux: Birds

Oui: Yes

La Petite École Internationale de Paris: The Little International School of Paris

Projet d'art: Art project

S'il vous plait: Please

Voilà: There it is

Meet the Author

Renee Beauregard Lute lives in the Pacific Northwest with one husband, two cats, and three amazing children. (Maddie, Simon, and Cecily, that's you!) There are many writers in the Pacific Northwest, and Renee is one of them. There may also be sasquatches in the Pacific Northwest, but Renee is not a sasquatch.

Like Winicker, Renee is from Western Massachusetts and loves macarons and sending postcards. Unlike Winicker, Renee has never lived in Paris, but she is very certain she would not hate it, even if Mirabel Plouffe lived next door.

Meet the Illustrator

Laura K. Horton is a freelance illustrator that has always had a passion for family, creativity and imagination. She earned her BFA in illustration and animation from the Milwaukee Institute of Art and Design. When she's not working, she can be found drinking tea, reading, and game designing. Recently she has moved to Espoo, Finland, to obtain a masters degree in game design and development.